A STATION F

SHORT
FUSE

ASH GREENSLADE

ISBN: 979-8646610868

By the Author

STATION HELIX SERIES

Station Helix
The Elzevir Collective
Torus

RYAN KERREK SERIES

Sinister Betrayal
Deadly Acquisition
Black Scarab
Hunting Caracal

FOR MORE ONLINE

Website: www.ashgreenslade.net
Twitter: @AshThrillers

SHORT

FUSE

1

FOUR HOURS AFTER MIDNIGHT and it's still comfortably warm in Pozzuoli. Lights are on in a handful of pastel-coloured apartment blocks on the road behind the harbour, but the old town is mostly at slumber. The waterfront is pleasant and characteristically Mediterranean, like you'd see on a tinted post-card from the 1960s, but being surrounded by a horseshoe of balconies and wooden shutters makes my counter-surveillance muscle twitch. We've been here for five nights in a row. I'm beginning to think my operation is blown.

My window is down. I can hear the metallic pings of halyards tapping against masts as sailboats rock lethargically in the breeze that's carrying hot air from the African coast. Dozens of pleasure craft are moored against the pontoons closest to our car park, and perhaps two hundred more behind the breakwaters on the northern edge of the bay, but Pozzuoli is also a ferry port servicing the Italian islands of Ischia and Procida. There's commerce here, but nothing on the scale of the vast container port at Naples, eight miles to the east.

Rocco Lanza glances at me from the driver's seat. He makes eye contact but says nothing. I can read the frustration at the inactivity in his eyes; I hope I'm masking my sense of irritation better than him. I turn away, focussing again on the iPad in my hands and the map on its screen.

I don't need to respond to Rocco's silent inquiry; I know he wouldn't expect me to. He might be prone to signs of boredom, but I'm still glad he's on my team, not least because he's a bilingual fourth-generation Italian from New York. Lanza served with the 75th Ranger Regiment before joining the CIA. I worked with those boys a few times when I was on military service; they're some of the best counter-terrorism warriors I've fought with.

We hadn't met before last week, but Lanza set a plan in motion from the Company's Rome office right after I called him from London, and I was impressed at how efficiently he liaised with the Agenzia Informazioni e Sicurezza Interna, Italy's Internal Security Service. He spared me the full details, but it seems the AISI were reluctant to let us take the lead on this mission until he persuaded them there wasn't time for dick measuring. They backed down and agreed to prepare a containment and evacuation strategy with the Italian Army. I hope it doesn't come to that.

In a perfect world the data about the plot would have gone straight to the Rome bureau, but intelligence gathering is never that linear. Information travels through a haphazard spider's web of informants, assets and operators. Sometimes it's given freely; more often it's intercepted. Rumours frequently originate from locations unconnected to the target. That's what happened this time – it was the first document that appeared on my new desk in London. Well, the first except the note about the tea club, and the *A to Z* some smartass left for me, opened on the Covent Garden page with a big red circle drawn around my building and a helpful *You Are Here* message.

And yeah, ideally I would be getting settled in as the new station chief, but it's not like I don't already know England's capital like the back of my hand (which I'm sure the joker knew). Besides, my no-nonsense deputy, Clare Quinn, has been there for two months already as acting chief since the last guy retired. I can rely on my straight-talking Texan colleague to hold the fort in my absence, and this Italian business demanded my attention. But, as I look at the clock in the corner of my iPad, I wonder again if I'm wasting my time here.

Lanza lifts his night-vision scope and directs it toward the tip of the southern breakwater, half a mile distant. "Might have something, Jack," he says. "Small vessel. Could be ours."

I follow his line of sight. It's too dark to make out the concrete structure itself, but I can see the boat's tiny deck lights against the night. I peer through my scope to get a better view. The tech cuts through the night and makes the image much clearer – grainy green through the lens. I frown. I might be wrong, but the vessel looks like a trawler, not the motor yacht we're here for. It chugs steadily into the harbour, not toward the pontoons near us, but on a bearing parallel to the dock wall.

"Caldwell to Lopez," I say into my covert radio.

"Go on, Jack," Eduardo 'Teddy' Lopez says in reply, keeping his voice quiet. He's south of our position, near the port master's building on the landward end of the breakwater.

"You see this?" I don't need to explain further.

"Yeah. Looks like they're mooring up alongside the wall. It's not Mughrib. But there's some activity down here I don't like. A blue or black Peugeot Boxer van and some guys riding around on scooters. They're heading down to the boat now."

The frown on my face deepens. I transmit again. "Okay, Teddy, keep me apprised. The intel might be wrong, or they could be on a different boat."

"Will do."

I lower my spotting scope and lean back against the seat. There's no reason other boats shouldn't be using the harbour, but *any* activity at four in the morning is suspicious in my book. I press my lips together in thought. A trawler could be bringing in catch from a late-night fishing run, I admit to myself, but the scooters Teddy clocked can't be explained away so easily. Or maybe they're just local kids who enjoy the thrill of racing through the town when the roads are dead. Could be, but I feel perturbed.

Eight minutes pass, and the only update over the comms is from Lopez, informing me that the Boxer has parked on the dock beside the fishing boat. The men he's seen have begun to unload some large plastic crates. They're heavy, and it's taking a while for them to be transferred into the panel van. Teddy reports that the guys on the scooters are no longer riding; they're helping the others shift the boxes.

"Descriptions?" I ask Lopez.

"Caucasians," he replies. "Must be local. I can't see anyone who looks African."

"Fine," I say in response. "Monitor them, Teddy."

Rocco makes a sweeping gesture towards the Golfo di Pozzuoli, pointing out more lights. It's impossible to gauge how far away they are; they're just somewhere between us and the harbours and hotels two miles distant on the other side of the bay. The trawler clearly isn't the only vessel on the water tonight, and I'm now worried that we're trying to run the operation with too few assets. There are dozens of places along the coastline where a boat could dock. I take a breath and think again about the intelligence which led us here.

While I'm dwelling on the strategy, Rocco concentrates on one of the boats he's spotted. I look up and realise it's definitely heading our way. Sensibly, he calls Eduardo on the comms for a second opinion. Lopez takes a moment and then confirms that, from his position, the vessel looks like our target; he has the clearest view of everything coming past the harbour wall. He adds that the Italians are still unloading crates from the trawler. The new arrival looks a lot more promising.

Energised, I begin to believe we've judged this right. The vessel we're looking for is a Nordhavn N60 motor yacht named Mughrib, registered in Tunisia. One of the Agency translators told me the name means 'sunset' in Tunisian Arabic. Compared to some luxury craft which sail the Mediterranean, Mughrib is definitely at the less conspicuous end of the scale, but nonetheless insanely expensive at over two million dollars. Sleeps eight in fine cabins, a dive platform at the stern, state-of-the-art navigation equipment – those sorts of specs. But, most importantly, the craft is a long-distance slugger, especially when her speed is kept to ten knots or below. Maybe that's why we've been waiting here for nearly a week.

Fares Bouzid – the owner of the boat – is rumoured to be an ISIS sympathiser. There's a CIA team in Tunisia scrutinising his background. He owns vast tracts of land on the Ras at-Taib peninsula, particularly around his home village of Sidi Daoud. My colleagues are at the early stage of their investigation, so it's not yet clear how he's made his money, but his status in the Tunisian Government could indicate corruption. To be fair, that's of no concern to the Company, but if he's supporting terrorist attacks against the West, we'll crush the fucker. If my operation is a success, it'll be the green light for decisive action against Bouzid.

I hear the whine of a scooter's engine from Via Roma – the road that skirts the harbour. Its headlight dances over the flat cobbles of the road, telling me the rider is weaving rather than travelling straight, but I've noticed the Italian kids have a propensity for this kind of showboating at any time of the day or night. The note of the engine changes as the vehicle slows down briefly, then there's a burst of power and it accelerates past us. It's moving quickly now, heading southward, but I can tell it's one of those high-power models, maybe a BMW C600, because there's plenty of room for the pillion passenger who's sitting up behind the driver and looking our way.

Rocco makes eye contact. "Busy here tonight," he remarks.

"Yeah." I tuck the iPad into the door compartment. I shift in my seat, uneasy. The harbour was deserted during the last four nights; now it feels like Piccadilly Circus. The holster containing my Glock 17 handgun moves a little under my jacket as I try to get comfortable. The weapon reminds me I'm supposed to maintain tactical control as the operation commander, but part of me wants to lead the raid when the time comes. But I have three guys in the back of the van for that; each one armed with an HK416 assault rifle and an assortment of other neat tools.

I look out at the harbour again from our spot in the car park. Mughrib is nudging against a pontoon, and a dark-skinned man with curly hair and a wispy beard jumps from the boat onto the floating platform. I watch as someone else tosses him a line from the yacht. He catches it and fastens it to a cleat, working efficiently and with obvious practised skill. It looks like he's wearing sandals, worn jeans and a puffa jacket. As soon as the boat is secure, the Tunisian hops back over the side and disappears into the cabin.

There's no other discernible movement on the pontoon or in the boat.

I activate my radio. "Status, Teddy?" I ask.

"Still have eyes on the trawler," Lopez replies. "Dunno what these guys are unloading, but I've counted eight crates and they're still working."

"Understood. Mughrib has docked. No activity though." I pause as a small Fiat car pulls off the road and crawls along the hardstanding toward the moorings. "Scrub that. We have a new arrival. White Fiat Punto. Stand by."

Lopez doesn't answer, leaving me to look at the car through my scope. The angle's wrong to see the number plate, but I can tell there are two male occupants. The image is sharp, and I realise that the night is retreating softly. It's still a while before sunrise, but the littoral view is slowly transforming in the pre-dawn greyness.

The bearded man reappears, struggling with what looks like a big plastic Pelican box. He steps off the boat as the Punto stops nearby. A second man comes from Mughrib's cabin, also carrying a heavy waterproof case.

Beside me, Lanza pulls a headphone set over his ears and aims a directional microphone at the boat and car. The Fiat's occupants stride over to the vessel, speak briefly with the boatmen, and lug away the proffered boxes. The conversation is brief, but it looks like Rocco has recorded at least some of it. He peels off the headphones as the newcomers heft the Pelicans into the trunk of the car.

"Arabic," he mutters. "No idea what they said."

I shrug. "Doesn't matter." I pause for a moment. "Update the AISI. Looks like we're moving."

Lanza nods, grabs his phone and calls a number on speed dial. He speaks as soon as the call is answered, then waits briefly as his message is acknowledged. He says, "Sì." The phone gets tucked away. He clutches the van's ignition key, ready to start the motor.

The Fiat driver and his mate are now back in the car. I watch as the small vehicle is manoeuvred on the dockside, ready to exit.

Part of me wishes we could intercept these bastards this minute, but we want the whole gang. Despite the quality of our intel – I'm now satisfied it was solid – we don't have the full picture. These guys are staging somewhere in Pozzuoli, but we don't yet know the location. There's a strong likelihood they have a backup plan. We could kill this one stone dead right now and seize the strontium-90, but that might not prevent another strike. This mission will only be a win if we find the vipers' nest and kill or capture every one.

"Caldwell to Stalker Team," I say into my comms.

A voice buzzes in my earpiece. "Go ahead."

"Looks like the target vehicle is about to leave the dock. White Fiat Punto. Can't give you the plate. We'll let it go and pull out once you confirm direction of travel."

"Understood, chief."

The Fiat moves past us and rejoins the road. I can hear its tyres drumming on the flat cobblestones.

"They're on the move," I announce. "All yours."

"We have eyes on." The radio falls silent.

I glance at Lanza. "Give it a minute."

He nods and fires up the ignition.

Lopez calls me with an update. "That Boxer just left the dock, Jack. Now out of view."

I know he's waiting for a decision. "Do you have the number?"

"Yes. And photos."

"Good job. But we'll leave that one for the locals. Send the images to the liaison desk." I pause for a moment. "The scooters?"

"Still buzzing around."

"Fine. The Italian authorities can deal with them. They're not our guys."

I don't need Lopez to track the Peugeot. It's a hunch, but I'm certain the lads he's been watching aren't connected to Mughrib and the Africans. Even if Fares Bouzid had shipped material on a second boat, there's no way he'd send it to the same dock on the same night as the first. I'm sure the Italians were unloading some kind of contraband, but that's not my problem.

Lanza flicks on the headlights, puts the van in gear and pulls out from our parking spot. But there's a commotion nearby, and a fraction of a second later I see scooter headlights racing toward us. Our path to the road is blocked in an instant. Rocco sees the firearms the moment I do, and I can tell he's tempted to plough through these yobs with our vehicle, but he thinks better of it.

I grab my Glock from beneath my jacket and chamber the first round. Suddenly there's gunfire outside, but the riders are firing into the air, not at us, like Wild West gunslingers raising Hell.

"Jack?" The urgent voice is in my earpiece, and I know it's one of the guys in the back.

"Local shits trying to intimidate us," I respond quickly. "Exit road. Deploy defensively but don't engage unless they shoot at *us*."

I hear the rear doors of the van burst open. Shadows rush past as my three guys move to the front of the vehicle with their HK416s. I pause briefly as they spread out and take up positions, using parked vehicles for tactical cover. I grab the door handle and slide out from the seat as Rocco does the same. He circles round the back of the vehicle and squats next to me. We face the crowd, using the engine block as a wall. I point my weapon in a two-handed grip at the nearest rider.

The gunfire stops, but we now have eight or nine handguns aimed in our direction – it's hard to know exactly how many adversaries we have because of the criss-crossing headlights. It's an absurd stalemate. I know what everyone's thinking. We have the firepower and training to cut these jerks down in seconds, but we have no desire to massacre Italian civilians, even if they're criminals. And they're posturing in front of us, guns tilted like in gangster movies, all attitude but fuck-all skill. I'm more nervous about the bravado that's keeping these boys from backing down than their bullets.

"Stalker Team to Caldwell," I hear in my comms. "You need backup?"

They caught my last transmission but don't know that we're

okay.

"Negative, negative!" I say. "Stay on mission!"

"Er... We've lost them, Jack."

What the fuck?

There's a follow-up transmission before I can reply. "We heard..." The comms drop off.

That's all it takes, I realise. A distraction for half a second can be enough to screw an entire operation. The consequences don't bear thinking about, but I have to pull this together somehow.

"Fucking find them again!" I shout back. "We'll deal with this mess."

I don't receive a reply from Stalker Team – they know I'm pissed off and there's nothing else to say. I just hope Teddy Lopez is picking up the slack. He's been smart enough to stay off the comms; he'll be monitoring and figuring out how to rebuild the strategy.

"Tell these fuckers to back down, Rocco!" I say to the man next to me.

Lanza responds right away, yelling something in Italian.

There's some jeering and nervous laughter from the scooter boys, but they don't move other than to make themselves look more menacing. They're probably shitting themselves, but no one wants to lose face among his mates.

This is ridiculous.

Lanza shouts again. My phrase-book Italian is inadequate to decipher his words, but his tone suggests he's using some fruity language. It doesn't do any good though – the barrier remains. It occurs to me that, if these guys are gangbangers, there's a good chance some of them have been snorting coke. If true, it just compounds the volatility of the confrontation. I just hope they haven't fried their brains too much to realise what will happen if one of them fires a shot in our direction.

Two more panel vans appear on the road and turn into the harbour, pulling up behind the group. The tension seems to lift a little; I guess these kids have been waiting for someone with authority to show up. Dawn is breaking now, and in the improving light I have a better view. Some figures disembark. I keep them in my peripheral vision, not wishing to distract myself from the yob who will take my first bullet. There's a quick confabulation between an older guy and one of the scooter riders.

After a few seconds, the old man steps forward. "English?" he calls out in an accented voice.

"American," I shout back. I don't want this to become a negotiation. By the look of it, neither does the Italian. I suspect he's as eager to avoid the police as I am. We need to bring this to a swift conclusion without bloodshed.

"You will not shoot," the man remarks. His English is clear but careful; educated rather than fluent.

I risk a quick glance in his direction. I'm surprised to see he appears frail and round-shouldered, but the authoritative tone in his voice seems to make up for any physical impairment. His hair is white and combed back.

"You need to back down!" I shout. "You're outgunned."

"Sì, but you will not shoot," he repeats.

I glance at Lanza. "Tell him to back off."

Rocco nods and calls out. He listens to the reply. "He says he can't."

"*What?*"

"Something about us jeopardising his operation."

"Tell him I couldn't care less about his contraband or whatever the fuck his boys have been doing here tonight."

Lanza shouts again, but I can tell the words aren't getting through.

Great. We're dealing with a fucking Camorra boss.

And then I hear words from the old man I can hardly believe. "Drop your weapons!"

I make eye contact with Rocco. "Tell me I heard that wrong."

He shakes his head. "Jack..."

I frown, rapidly assessing my options. The Italian is right – I will not order my men to murder these sons of bitches. We could drag out this standoff until the police get here – which I can't imagine will be very long – but a bilious feeling in my gut tells me these gangbangers would be keener for a gunfight with the cops than us. Even if the police could contain this screwed-up incident, we'd be detained and locked up until some government suit negotiated our release, and that could take days.

I lower my gun.

"Stand down." The order tastes bitter on my tongue. I repeat the words to emphasise my decision. "Stand down. Lopez knows where we are. He'll regroup with Stalker Team."

I don't get any pushback because my guys are loyal and obedient, but I'm furious with myself for having to give the order. I don't have a choice. I'm relying on this mob boss to act rationally, hoping he won't execute us under the scrutiny of the harbour's CCTV cameras. But I can't predict where this is going.

"Set the guns down, boys," I mutter. "Know when to hold 'em, know when to fold 'em."

I crouch down and put my Glock on the concrete.

2

Sᴇᴄᴏɴᴅs ᴀғᴛᴇʀ ᴏᴜʀ ʀᴇʟᴜᴄᴛᴀɴᴛ sᴜʀʀᴇɴᴅᴇʀ, we're marched to the vans and forced into the cargo compartments. We're shoved onto the floor, face down. I'm surprised that we're not tied up, but it's obvious the Italians want to flee the port without delay. I find myself lying between two of my assault team guys. I assume Rocco Lanza and the third rifleman are now in the other vehicle. Some gang members climb in, and I hear the doors slamming shut. In moments we're on the move. It's only then that someone frisks us. The search is superficial but good enough to find the handguns my colleagues are carrying, and all our cell phones. I silently acknowledge that putting us prone on the floor of the van is a clever move, even without restraints.

My guess that we're heading for one of the sink estates in Naples where these clans operate is swiftly proved wrong when the van jerks to a halt just three minutes later. The doors are yanked open and, in the dawn light, I see we're outside a Roman ruin. There's a rusty metal fence around the entire structure to keep out trespassers, but I notice that someone in the group has a key for the main gate.

Knowing we can't have left Pozzuoli – I can still smell the salty breeze from the harbour – I try to figure out where it is they've brought us. I'm relieved we've not been smuggled deep into Camorra territory, like the forlorn and foreboding concrete jungle of Le Vele di Scampia, or another of the slums where drug misuse is rife. Italy might be beloved by tourists, but there are some ghettos which are more degraded, crumbling and poverty-stricken than even the harshest Soviet-era districts in Russia and Eastern Europe.

The rising sun casts a warm sandy glow on the ancient walls. The curved structure has collapsed in many places but it's still enormous. Great archways make up the perimeter, interrupted only by broad flights of stone steps which appear to lead to the sky. Trees surround the building, partly shielding it from the ring road. As we're hurried through a gap into the interior, I remember reading about this site – it's the Pozzuoli Amphitheatre, the third largest arena of its type in Italy, and almost two millennia old.

Someone puts his hand on my shoulder and gives me a shove. I don't react to the provocation but use the moment to glance around. We're beneath the stands now, following an ancient passageway through the building toward the arena floor. The air smells earthy but not stale. Emerging through a small archway, I find myself in a vast oval space, roughly forty yards wide and double that in length. Despite my predicament, I feel awe at my surroundings. Even though the seating is worn and strewn with weeds, it's easy to imagine what this place was like in the time of the gladiators.

Rocco Lanza and the others are nearby. I'm thankful that the strike team is still intact, even though we're in no position to fight back, but the casual way the Italians are waving their pistols in the air continues to sour my mood. I risk a look over my shoulder. The old man with the white hair is following the group, shuffling along rather than walking with purpose. I surmise that he's definitely ill, and yet I can't help but admire his bearing. The scooter punks might be full of bluster, but their deference to this man is clear in their eyes.

But it's the woman he's conversing with who really draws my attention. Even though her dark hair is tied back in a harsh ponytail, and she's wearing a charcoal grey fleece, black hiking trousers and boots, the plain clothes and stern expression can't hide her classical Italian beauty. I wonder if she and the old man are related. I get pushed again, harder this time, so I turn my head away and continue across the dusty ground.

The light is stronger now, reflecting on the modern metal grilles which have been placed down the centre of the arena to cover an underground corridor, running from one end to the other. There are dozens more hatches spread evenly around the oval near the arena walls, and I realise their purpose is to allow daylight to illuminate a subterranean passageway which circles beneath our feet. The design of the amphitheatre is incredible; I just wish I could enjoy it without some teenage villain pointing a gun between my shoulder blades. The only silver lining is knowing that if Eduardo Lopez and Stalker Team hit this place when it's closed to the public, innocent civilians won't be killed in the cross-fire. In truth, though, a rescue mission isn't the priority. My crew and I are expendable. Lopez must thwart the terror attack.

I'm pushed toward a gap in the wall. Lichen-covered steps lead to the chamber below the arena. Much of the interior is still in shadow, but there's enough light now for me to see it. The pattern of archways I saw outside is replicated down here but on a smaller scale, creating a line of alcoves. The corridor curves to match the outline of the ground above, so I can only see six or seven arches in either direction. I feel like I'm standing in the world's biggest wine cellar, but I know these spaces were used to hold lions and gladiators. There are pieces of fluted columns lying on the ground, clearly damaged and moved from their original positions.

The old man gives an order; his minions herd me and my team into an alcove. There's no cover here at all – if the mob guys shoot, we're all fucked. I try to listen to the conversation the boss is having with the woman and two senior underlings. I hear the subordinates address the frail man as Don Ciro a few times, but I can't under-stand anything else. My miniature collection of Italian phrases is useless. I'm doing my best to pick out words to no avail. I realise they're probably using the Neapolitan language, not Italian. I glance at Rocco. I can tell from his expression that he's struggling to interpret the speech.

Eventually the man named Ciro steps closer. The woman stands beside him, and for a moment we lock eyes. She is stunning. It takes all my willpower to turn away when the old man speaks.

"Who is the leader?" Ciro asks in English, looking directly at me.

20

I step forward. "I am."

He nods slowly. "Americans with guns. Why are you in Pozzuoli?"

I don't answer.

He gives an instruction in Neapolitan. Two men step forward and drag me from the alcove. One of them unfastens and removes my jacket. He tosses it onto the floor. My gun holster is empty, so he doesn't bother unstrapping it, but he rams a punch into my stomach as his mate grabs my head and bends me forward. The assault doesn't do me any damage, but a flash of anger courses through my veins, and I have to force myself not to retaliate. The Italian turns my head sharply. I realise he's not trying to injure me – he's checking my ears for an earpiece. He lets me go and faces the old man. He nods.

Ciro says, "Take it out."

I fish the tiny device from my ear canal. One of my assailants grabs it and tosses it onto the floor.

Ciro looks at it for a moment and then grinds it beneath his boot. "Spiare," he says with venom. I don't need him to translate. He speaks to his men once more, and seconds later my entire crew is being searched for covert communication equipment. They find all the devices and destroy them. The others are shoved back into the alcove. I make eye contact with the leader once again.

"You need to let us go," I tell him, glowering.

He shakes his head. "It is too late for that." He pauses. "Why are American spies interested in my business?"

"I'm *not* interested in your business. I'm not here for you."

"Really?" Ciro makes a gesture and utters someone's name.

A swarthy thug with a barrel chest and a greasy quiff steps out from another chamber, leading Eduardo Lopez by the arm. There's a large graze on Teddy's cheek, and the skin around his eye is swollen. Dried blood stains his lips and chin.

Shit.

Teddy's been roughed up, but he's endured worse from harder men. He even cracks a sly grin in my direction, but we both know there's nothing to joke about.

"Then why was your man watching my boat?" Ciro asks.

I shake my head. "You're mistaken. Your operation is of no concern to us."

Ciro shrugs. "Perhaps. But you have seen us. You will tell the police."

I give a short mirthless laugh. "You probably *own* the police."

A smile forms on the old man's lips but fades quickly. "Why were you in the harbour?"

"I can't tell you. But it was not for you."

Ciro turns round and looks at the woman. "Alessandra?"

She stares at me for a moment but quickly looks away, bowing her head for a private conversation with Ciro. Suddenly she takes three steps toward me.

"You need to talk to my father," she snaps. There's a strong accent, but she's confident with the English language. "This will not end well if you refuse."

I shake my head. "I've told you already – I'm not interested in his business."

She nods. "Yes, you said that. But you did not say why you *are* here."

"That's right. And it will stay that way."

Alessandra leans forward, and I find myself staring at her dark eyes. "You don't understand," she says emphatically. "I can't help you if you remain silent."

I concentrate on her face for twenty seconds without speaking. I can't tell if she's just digging for intel or whether she's trying to stop the old man murdering us.

She breaks the silence. "You're CIA."

I don't answer.

"My father was right." Alessandra steps back. "You're helping the Italian authorities against the clans. You're a spy."

This conversation is going nowhere. If I screw this up, my men are dead. I control my breathing, forcing myself to work the angles. Reluctantly, I know I must give some ground.

22

"Your name is Alessandra, right?"

"Sì," she replies, holding my gaze.

"Well, Alessandra, only one part of your theory can be correct."

She frowns. "Explain."

"American operatives have one purpose: to protect US citizens. Your little empire might be a thorn in the side of the Italian police, but you're insignificant to me and my team."

Alessandra considers my words. "So, you're not interested in the Spada family?"

"I'd never heard of you before today. You can go back to your drug-running and human-trafficking for all I care. Let us go and you'll never see us again."

She frowns at me. "Perhaps you speak the truth. But my father isn't so trusting. That's why he's still the boss." She walks back to Ciro, says something under her breath, and strides away along the subterranean corridor.

I grimace. I thought I was getting through to her, but now it seems she's washed her hands of the situation and doesn't want to be around for the consequences.

Ciro Spada looks at me again. "Nothing personal," he says. The words sound almost kind. "But I cannot take the risk." He follows his daughter. He calls out an instruction in his native language. Some gangbangers step closer to the alcove, blocking our way out, aiming their handguns at me and my crew.

Think, Jack!

Somehow one final idea bursts through my brain. It's not just power and money the Camorra lust after, I realise. They want respect.

"Don Ciro!" I shout out, hoping the honorific will encourage him to think again.

The man halts his shuffling steps, turns slowly and stares at me. He lifts his hand. The gunmen relax their shoulders and lower the guns. Ciro holds my gaze, clearly expecting me to speak. I wonder if he's been waiting for this all along.

"We're here to stop a terror attack," I explain hurriedly. "Many people – *Italians* – will die if you don't let us complete our mission."

I'm not sure if he's understood everything I've said, but Alessandra has returned. They converse once more. After a few seconds they walk back to me. I notice their arms are linked. She's supporting her father; it looks as though the effort is tiring him.

"My name is Jack Caldwell," I continue. I'm about to reveal information that could put me in jail, but I don't have a choice. "I wasn't in the harbour to watch your boat. I was there for the motor yacht. She was delivering two cases of radioactive material from Tunisia. The terrorists are building a dirty bomb." I pause. "You know what that is?"

Alessandra nods.

I gesture toward the scooter riders. "Your boys stopped us from pursuing the targets. Our plan was to locate their staging post and then take them out before they could arm and deploy the device."

Alessandra translates quickly for her father.

He stares at me as he listens to the words. There's a pained expression on his face as he speaks in English. "Where is the bomb?"

"Right now? I have no idea. But their target is the Naples American High School."

Alessandra frowns. "That's a protected facility. They'll never get past the security points."

"They don't need to get inside," I answer fast. "It's a symbolic target. Kids of NATO personnel deployed in Italy study there. Attacking the school is a crusade against the United States and all her allies. The terrorists will detonate the explosives nearby. Their intention is not to bring down the building, it's to fill the air with radioactive particles." I pause for a moment. "And it will be the schoolkids who are exposed first."

Alessandra looks aghast. "Like poison?"

"Long-term health issues. Cancer. Heart and breathing problems. Slow deaths."

"How bad?"

I assume she's referring to the fallout. I shake my head. "Hard to say. Two or three square kilometres contaminated as an absolute minimum. If the wind shifts, the dust could blow across other parts of Naples too."

"Many people will fall ill?"

"Yes, but the physical damage is not the only purpose of a dirty bomb."

"What do you mean?"

"They want to cause fear and economic chaos. The cost of decontamination would be millions of dollars. This region of Italy would lose its tourism and freight commerce overnight."

Alessandra turns from me and puts her arm around Ciro's shoulders. They talk frantically. Finally, she faces me again.

"My father finds this story hard to believe."

I glare at him while answering her. "Tell your father he's a fucking idiot."

Ciro Spada stares at me for a few seconds in astonishment. He might not be fluent in English but he's sure understood that. A broad smile spreads across his face.

"Men rarely speak to me in that way," he intones.

"I don't give a shit. Are you going to let us go now? So we can prevent the attack on your city?"

He holds my gaze. "How will you stop it?"

The question floors me. I don't have an answer. Stalker Team lost their quarry, and I have no idea if they found the Fiat Punto again.

"Give me my phone," I say, glancing at the broken radios on the floor. "I need to call my men."

Ciro barks an order. A young lad jumps forward and hands me my smartphone. I activate the screen and see that I've got one bar of signal strength. I scroll through my contacts and dab the icon next to a name.

My call is answered in seconds. I know Johnny Coleman wants to speak, but I cut him off.

"Shut up, Johnny. Did you find the vehicle?"

I groan when he tells me no, but I'm relieved when he announces that Stalker Team snapped a few photos. He confirms he's logged the registration plate. It's the best news I've heard all week.

"Send me the images then wait for my next instruction," I say, ending the call.

Ten seconds later, my phone beeps. I quickly open an image file. It's not a great photo, but it reveals the number and a crack in the rear off-side light cluster.

I look at Ciro and Alessandra, showing them the screen. "That's the car we were trying to follow from the harbour. You need to let us go right now so we can search for it."

Ciro's understood enough. He shakes his head. "A white Fiat Punto in an Italian city?" he remarks. I see his point. He turns to Alessandra and makes a comment in Neapolitan.

She grins and looks at me. "My father has decided not to kill you."

I raise my eyebrows. "I'm grateful."

"But only because the CIA and the Spada clan will forge a temporary alliance." She pauses. "You must help my father save Pozzuoli and Naples."

I try, but I can't contain my smile. The old man has figured out how to make himself a local hero. I nod at her, knowing now is the time to let the mob boss take charge.

Ciro Spada faces his men, holding up my phone. I don't need a translator to figure out he's reciting the registration plate and describing the damaged light cluster. Most of the scooter boys dash for the exits, leaving just half a dozen gang members, Ciro himself and his stunning daughter.

"Don Ciro has promised five thousand euros to the first man who finds the car," Alessandra explains. "Better than your surveillance, no? They will search every corner of the city. They will call us when it is found."

I give her a half-smile. "I hope your plan works, Alessandra. Because we have only two hours before the school opens."

3

THE SHADOWS ON THE ARENA FLOOR are in retreat as we make our way out from the catacombs and return to the vehicles. The morning is bright. There's no hint of the sea breeze, and the day is already feeling hot beneath a hazy bleached sky. Someone has driven our surveillance van up from the harbour. It stands behind a silver Volkswagen Tiguan outside the metal fence. The panel vans which brought us here are further along the street. I glance up and down the road and see several parked cars; it's obvious that the heavyset thugs standing next to them are Ciro's senior henchmen.

The Camorra boss faces me when we're outside the gate. He gestures at the group. "Divide your men with mine. You will stay with Alessandra. She is in charge."

The notion of splitting my team infuriates me, but I know I don't have a choice. I'm less put out by the prospect of spending time with Alessandra Spada.

Ciro offers his hand. "You are a lucky man, Jack Caldwell of the CIA."

There isn't much strength in his handshake; his fingers feel bony in my grip. I look at him for a moment before replying. There's sadness in his mien which I hadn't noticed before, as though he knows he's a weaker self of the man he once was, and is now trying too hard to stave off a pitiful fate. I feel sympathy for his plight. I wonder if those eyes are trying to hide a sense of humiliation. I'm sure Ciro Spada would rather lose his empire to a rival cartel in a territorial battle than through the irreversible decline of his health.

I try to keep my tone respectful. "Grazie, Don Ciro."

He nods, turns away and ambles towards the Tiguan. A minder

opens a door for him, but Ciro calls out to the rest of the group before settling into the vehicle. I can't understand his command, but I sense its meaning when he refers to his daughter as Donna Alessandra. From the affirmative signals he receives, it's obvious that this isn't the first time she's taken charge. I realise that the destiny of the Spada clan lies with her, and Ciro has been moulding her to take his place in the hierarchy.

The VW drives away moments later. Alessandra immediately starts barking orders and gesticulating in the Italian fashion to emphasise her words. It's clear that she's allocating her clan members to the various vehicles parked in the street, and I realise after a few moments that she's indicating which of my men should accompany hers. My guys don't move, glancing at me for confirmation. Reluctantly, I nod to affirm Alessandra's instructions. I can tell she wants to get moving immediately. It's a sentiment we share. The road outside the amphitheatre is becoming busy as the day wakes up, and we're at risk of drawing attention to ourselves if we hang around much longer.

Alessandra steps closer to me and prods my arm to guide me toward a grey Seat MPV. I frown, but she either ignores it or doesn't notice. We sit in the rear seats and tug the doors shut. Two clan boys jump in the front. The passenger shifts himself around so he can watch me, evidently tasked with protecting Alessandra. From the way he's keeping his hand inside his jacket, I'm certain he has a handgun concealed there.

The convoy pulls out and loops around the ancient arena. The road is narrow, with the historical site's metal fence on one side and three- and four-storey apartment blocks on the other. The buildings are painted in peach and ochre pastels. Here, as down by the harbour, the individual residences all have balconies and wooden shutters. Some blocks have rows of shops occupying the ground level. I notice a pair of cyclists out for an early ride. We drive up an incline. I spot a handful of commercial units with metal roller shutters, and there's a load of graffiti painted on some grubby walls. I suspect a lot of the buildings were constructed before the Second World War, but it's hard to judge. We pass under a railway bridge. Without my iPad I don't know where we are, but the driver clearly has a destination in mind.

I'm usually an excellent navigator; my internal compass tends to know what direction I'm facing. But it's a challenge in a place like Pozzuoli because the town's a labyrinth. Roads twist and turn in deference to the rugged volcanic landscape. I try to recall the maps and satellite images I studied when preparing for the mission. I remember there are some patches of high open ground and nature reserves between the eastern fringes of Pozzuoli and the western suburbs of Naples where the American High School is located. I guess we're somewhere in between, but most of the flat land is occupied, and the smaller town more or less blends in with the city. We must be less than half a mile from the sea, but I can't see the coastline because of the buildings everywhere on the contoured landscape.

After a few minutes the convoy pulls off the main road and scurries up a dusty track before halting in a cobbled courtyard outside a rustic house. It's one of the most attractive buildings I've seen since I've been here. It's surrounded by an old wall. Foliage tumbles over the boundary. There's a strong floral smell in the warm air as we step out of the MPV. But, as I glance around, I notice the lovely old house overlooks commercial sprawl in the valley below. The scene diminishes the character of the place, making it feel forlorn.

Alessandra walks with me to my surveillance van and allows me to retrieve my iPad. I load the mapping application and finally get my bearings. I realise that the circuitous route we've had to take to get to this remote location amounts to only half a mile as the crow flies. The school is still roughly two thirds of a mile to the east. It's a good spot to use as a rendezvous point.

Alessandra makes eye contact. "Phone your Stalker Team. Tell them to meet us here."

I wish she wouldn't speak to me in instructions, but I'm glad she's willing to let us regroup. I make the phone call and read out the name of the road from the digital map. They're not far away, and Johnny informs me it will take about ten minutes to travel from their current location. I take some reassurance from the fact that I'm reassembling my team, even though we've lost the trail of the bombers. There's something in Alessandra's confident demeanour which makes me think we will actually track down the scum.

Every operation evokes the sentiment of being slightly detached from reality, but what I'm seeing now is something entirely new and unexpected. The Italians who were ready to execute us in the amphitheatre are now content to return our kit to us, including our HK416 assault rifles. We seem to have reached an unspoken understanding – we're operating on their turf by their rules, but the clan members know that we're the specialists who have the skill to stop the terrorists. They observe my operators with curiosity and, unless I'm mistaken, some degree of admiration. My nervousness at this peculiar truce hasn't evaporated, although Alessandra has grasped the gravity of the threat against her countrymen. She's in total control of her guys. She lets us work while we wait for Johnny and the rest of the team, asking the occasional question but not getting in our way.

The Stalker Team van crawls up the lane and pulls into the courtyard. The frowns on my guys' faces are obvious through the windscreen, but I wave them over as they disembark. I wait for them to form a semicircle around me before I speak.

"We've acquired some local help," I state. That's all the explanation they'll get for now. "There are teams searching for the Punto as we speak," I continue. "We'll know the moment they find it. Get your kit ready."

I don't wait for questions. Johnny and his team return to their van. I know they have some weapons in the back, but they're also holding most of the surveillance kit, including miniature drones, infrared and thermal imaging cameras, and some neat devices which pick up cell signals and replicate the function of phone masts so we can eavesdrop on live calls. We never know exactly what gear we will need, so we tend to bring the lot.

I might be calmer now, but my impatience is testing me. Getting the equipment ready is vital, but without a target we're just biding our time in a fog of frustration. I ought to know better – I've taken part in hundreds of missions and experienced countless delays – but this one feels unique. Or perhaps I'm just annoyed that a perfectly good surveillance strategy unravelled so fast. Maybe I should have pulled in more resources. And next time I won't overlook the possibility of local hoodlums screwing up my plan.

I draw breath and try to focus. Now isn't the time to beat myself up over what-ifs. I look up and see Alessandra studying my face. I wonder if she can read my thoughts.

When she says, "Are you okay?" I draw the firm conclusion that yes, she can.

I shrug. "Strange day."

Her face lights up with a smile. She's more of a distraction than my self-pity. "For me too," she says, but I'm not sure exactly what she means. She takes my arm and leads me gently toward the edge of the road. We stand together, our backs to the activity in the courtyard, overlooking the valley and its modern industrial units. The contrast between the wooded hillsides and the commerce is stark. "The American school is that way," she says, pointing.

This time I can read what she's telling me. It's a crowded town with a sizeable population. She's not letting it show outwardly, but I know she fears the aftermath of a dirty bomb explosion in her neighbourhood.

I try to reassure. "If your men are as good as I think they are, we'll find the terrorists." My brief speech probably doesn't convey as much positivity as I'd like, and I'm not sure I believe my own words. But Alessandra looks at me with a soft expression, understanding what I'm attempting to say.

She turns away and stares across the valley. "They will call. The bombers are not far away."

Her statement is more than wishful thinking; it's a distinct likelihood that she's right. I can tell from her expression that she's evaluated the situation tactically, not just uttered vague speculation. I agree with her; the terrorists will have established a nearby bolthole so they can minimise risks. I assume that Ciro reached the same conclusion and directed several of his scooter boys to concentrate their efforts around the vicinity of the school. The Africans are almost certainly within a mile of the target right now. I frown. That's still a huge radius.

Alessandra speaks again. "Are you returning to the US when this is over?" The question catches me off-guard.

"London, actually," I reply.

She raises her eyebrows in surprise. "You have a CIA office there?" she probes.

I grin. "I don't recall confirming that's my line of work."

Alessandra smiles back. "No, you didn't. Not directly, anyway." She places her hand on my chest. "But I'd expect that from a professional."

She withdraws her hand almost at once and turns away before I can reply. Not that I know what to say in response to her comment. I follow her back to the courtyard, realising that one of her men has called her name. The Italian is holding out a phone to her.

Alessandra grabs the mobile. "Sì?" The conversation is brief. "Molto bene," she says before ending the call. She locks eyes with me. "They found the car."

The words feel like sunlight bursting through clouds, but it's time to go to work, not celebrate. I signal to Rocco, Teddy and Johnny to join me and Alessandra in the shade of the house. I fire up the iPad's mapping application as Alessandra announces that the white Punto is parked in a residential street in the Bagnoli quarter.

I find the area on the screen and zoom in. I determine that Bagnoli is a small district which, from a bird's-eye view, looks like a slice of pie. The shallow curve of its northern border runs alongside train tracks. Another edge meets the sea, and a road called Via

Bagnoli marks the south-eastern limit of the region, linking the beach to the railroad. Contained within the wedge shape are numerous residential streets laid out in a fairly regular grid pattern. I can see that the district is roughly two thirds of a mile south of the high school.

Alessandra takes the iPad from me and types in the target street's name, saving me from guessing its spelling. "Apartment blocks," she states. "Usually three or four levels. Narrow streets. Lots of parked vehicles." She dabs the screen. "That's where the car is. But I can't tell you which address."

I hold her gaze. "Thank you. It's a start." I make eye contact with Rocco Lanza. "Rocco, check the licence plate with the authorities. I'm not expecting it to be registered locally, but it's worth a shot."

Lanza nods and steps away from the group, reaching for his phone.

"What do you think, Johnny?" I say to my Stalker Team leader.

Johnny Coleman takes a moment to study the tablet. "The grid helps. We can deploy in a couple of spots to monitor the car without trouble. But identifying the apartment will be more problematic." He pauses. "They might have abandoned the car, Jack."

He's making a good point. I'd felt relief when the Spada clan located the Punto; now I realise I've overlooked the possibility that the Africans could be holed up elsewhere.

I call out to Lanza, interrupting his phone conversation. "Find out if there's any CCTV in that street."

Rocco nods and waves, acknowledging my order.

I make eye contact with Alessandra again. "We're looking for North Africans. Is Bagnoli the sort of place where they might stay unnoticed?"

She presses her lips together in thought. "Yes, I suppose so. There is an immigrant population there. Apartments are not so expensive to rent. People come and go. They have little money."

Lanza returns. "Negative on the licence. Fake plate. And there's no CCTV."

"Damn it." I look again at the map. I notice a collection of apartment complexes on the north side of the rail tracks. "What about here?" I ask Alessandra.

"I know this place," she replies slowly. "I don't think so. The neighbourhood is more open, even though the blocks are bigger. The parking compounds are secure and can be seen easily from every window. Not so good for working in secret."

I realise the terrorists could be anywhere if they have abandoned the Fiat Punto. Speculating about random locations across the city is pointless. But... There's a stray thought floating around my head, and I can't grasp it. I try to focus.

Alessandra sees the doubt in my eyes and places her hand on my forearm. Her touch is electric and instantly calming. "What are you thinking, Jack?" she asks, her voice almost a whisper.

It's enough to grab that thought fragment and pin it down. Somehow this woman is making a connection with me. I don't understand how she's doing it. I lock eyes with her. "They're near the car," I say with confidence.

"How do you know this?" Alessandra questions. She isn't doubting my statement; she's making me work through it logically. It helps.

"The intelligence stated that they would deploy within hours of receiving the strontium-90 from Mughrib. They had to move the material to their staging post first. It's heavy – they would need to do it fast or they'd get noticed. They also need time to construct the bomb. They're against the clock. They need to drive to the school and park the vehicle before the staff arrive." I pause. "They *do* have a second vehicle, but the Punto is still in play."

Alessandra regards me thoughtfully. "Why?"

"Because this isn't a suicide mission. The Tunisians will not hang around to irradiate themselves. They need to flee back down to the harbour and board the boat." I pause. "They're in the neighbourhood where your guys found the car."

Johnny speaks next. "Let's get down there, Jack. We can use the Insects."

He's referring to the miniature drones in the back of the surveillance van. We have four of them; state-of-the-art CIA tech worth ten thousand dollars apiece. The drones are smaller than golf balls. They have high-definition cameras which operate on a wide dynamic range, meaning they can cope with bright and dark conditions simultaneously, like the human eye. We can fly the little electronic critters through sunlight and shadow and still receive a clear image. It'll take a while to peer through every window in the street, but with all four in the air at once, we should cover each apartment block in minutes.

Using the map, I direct my assets to take up positions in the roads near the Punto's location. Alessandra translates rapidly for the benefit of her men. She still believes this is a joint operation. I suppose she has a point, but when we have the target address, the Spada cartel will have to stay out of our way. For now, I'm glad to make use of the local knowledge.

Thirty seconds later, our vehicles pull out of the rustic courtyard. Next to me in the back of the Seat MPV, Alessandra glances my way. "Do you think we will stop them?"

I smile at her. "If we find the apartment, it's all over for these guys."

"You will shoot them?"

My smile fades. "It's a capture-or-kill mission. If we take them alive, we can interrogate them later for more intel. But the safety of my men is the priority. If the Africans don't comply..."

I let the words trail off.

Alessandra nods. "I would kill them," she says, her tone neutral. I believe her.

Soon we're on the Via San Gennaro Agnano; a continuation of the road which brought us from Pozzuoli. A view of the sea appears on my right as we head toward the Bagnoli district. The water looks flat calm beneath an azure sky. I lose sight of the ocean as the road descends through high banks of trees, but it's there again a moment later, and I can see a small island just off the coast and piers stretching out from a bay. We divert briefly from the coastline – I conclude that it's impossible to get from one place to another directly in Italy – and after a few more turns and junctions we're in the heart of the residential quarter.

The vehicles split up and find their designated parking spots in the Bagnoli streets, but I want to satisfy myself that the white Punto is still where Ciro's men found it. I ask Alessandra to speak to our driver. Moments later we're moving at twenty miles per hour between square apartment blocks. The target car is tucked against a pavement. We take another turn and the driver pulls in, stopping twenty yards from the junction.

The Stalker Team boys get the Insects into the air within minutes. I alternate between the camera streams on my iPad as the miniature drones dart around the buildings, creep up to window ledges and even intrude through open shutters. Alessandra stares at the screen, evidently impressed with the clarity of the images. I'm sure we're breaking all kinds of Italian surveillance laws, but I don't really give a shit, and we're here in collaboration with the Security Service, anyway. We don't have the time or inclination to pry into the lives of ordinary Italian citizens, but we do need to track down the terror cell.

It takes thirty-seven minutes. One of the drone operators pilots the device onto a window ledge and gets a view of a suspect. The angle is partly obscured due to a net curtain, but I'm convinced the black male in the apartment is one of the guys from the harbour. I watch as the drone ascends a couple of inches, moves to the left and settles back down. The room is sparsely furnished. I can see a few plastic tubs and an assortment of tools on a small table. The corner of what looks like a Pelican case occupies a sliver of the screen. As I watch, another man crosses in front of the camera. He, too, is black African.

I lean back in my seat. "It's them."

Alessandra doesn't speak. She knows it's my rodeo now. Without the covert radio network, I have to do this by phone, but our cells have an encrypted conference function which works well enough. For a moment I visualise the tunnel beneath the Roman amphitheatre, remembering how Ciro's henchman crushed the earpieces underfoot. I smile at the distraction, knowing how easily this could have gone another way, but I don't dwell on the thought.

I ensure that Teddy Lopez and Rocco Lanza have the rear door of the block covered as discreetly as possible – there's always a strong chance that hyper-vigilant terrorists will detect something's screwed and make a run for it. Four of Alessandra's men loiter a short way down the street smoking cigarettes, evidently keen to get involved if they can. I'm reluctant to allow it, but I'm confident that Teddy and Rocco will put down the enemy long before the Italians can even draw their weapons.

Johnny Coleman works the lock on the front door, popping it open as quietly as he can, clearing the path for Strike Team. Clad in drab grey military gear, they appear from nowhere and slide into the building like ghosts. I know this won't take long.

The commotion begins twenty seconds later. Even from the street outside, I can hear an internal door being smashed open. Two flash-bangs go off – loud enough to make Alessandra jump; bright enough to illuminate the windows despite the daylight. And then there's gunfire – the distinctive rhythmic cracks as the HK416 rifles unleash controlled bursts.

The silence of the aftermath is eerie, but I wait for my guys to tell me their status, rather than chase them for an update. I'm informed that five terrorists are eliminated. A sixth – found cowering behind a wardrobe – has been detained. Most importantly, the strontium-90 and the explosives are now secure.

I call Lanza's name over the open comms. "Get on the line to the Italians, Rocco."

"On it, boss," he replies. "And I'll get the coastguard to seize the motor yacht."

I dab the screen of the iPad, switching off the camera feed, and lean against the seat. "Good job, guys," I say into my phone. "We'll hold the fort until the authorities arrive. Then we'll regroup and leave town." I smile to myself for a moment, then add: "Assuming the Spadas let us go."

Alessandra twists around in her seat and grins at me. "I think we shall allow that." She pauses. "Give me your phone."

A frown crosses my lips. I end the conference call. I'm not sure why I do it, but I place the mobile in her hands.

Alessandra touches the screen to access my contact list. She keys in a number using the on-screen keyboard, saves it and presses the dial graphic. Her phone rings a few seconds later. She ends the call and returns my phone.

"So, you're leaving today?" she asks, staring at me.

I nod. "It's the way we roll."

She shrugs. "I suppose so. But you haven't eaten in hours. My uncle owns a nice restaurant near the harbour." She looks at me intently. "Will you have breakfast with me?"

I hold her gaze. "Sure. I'd like that, Alessandra."

"Call me Alessa." She reaches for the door handle. "I must speak to my men and call my father. He'll be happy we found the terrorists."

"Please send my regards to Don Ciro. And my thanks."

"I will." She pushes open the door, steps out and turns to face me. "We work well together, Jack."

From the mischievous glint in her eyes, I don't think she's referring to hunting terrorists. I return her smile. "Sì, Alessa. We do."

Author's Note

THANK YOU for reading SHORT FUSE. I hope you enjoyed the book. Although the story is set before the STATION HELIX novels, it was actually written after the RYAN KERREK spin-off series. SHORT FUSE links to the chapter in TORUS when Jack Caldwell visits Alessandra Spada. I always wondered how they had met, and how Jack had persuaded Alessandra's father not to kill him. That mystery is now solved!

STATION HELIX SERIES

Station Helix
The Elzevir Collective
Torus

RYAN KERREK SERIES

Sinister Betrayal
Deadly Acquisition
Black Scarab
Hunting Caracal

FOR MORE ONLINE

Website: www.ashgreenslade.net
Twitter: @AshThrillers

Printed in Great Britain
by Amazon

58130096R00031